By

Larry J. Gunter

This book is a work of non-fiction. Names and places have been changed to protect the privacy of all individuals. The events and situations are true.

ISBN: 1-4140-0394-3 (e-book)
ISBN: 1-4140-0393-5 (Paperback)

Library of Congress Control Number: 2003098668

This book is printed on acid free paper.

Printed in the United States of America
Bloomington, IN

1stBooks – rev. 01/14/04

First Experience

Pit

It was a hot summer Friday in 1985 and as always there was absolutely nothing to do. Growing up in the southern streets of a South Carolina city didn't always produce the opportunities to get in trouble. But still, given enough time, we had a way of finding trouble. Or, should I say, it had a way of finding us.

The last four summers I had spent in New York with my cousins. But this year money was tight and I took odd jobs to make extra money. Since I was only a youngster, I couldn't get your regular nine-to-five, so I had to settle for jobs like mowing lawns and washing cars. The money wasn't the best, but I was only ten years old with no bills. The lack of responsibilities made it easy for me to save up for school clothes.

Like clockwork, around three o'clock every afternoon my friend

Pit

Mike would come by to see if he could cash in on a meal. Sometimes he just wanted to see what kind of trouble we could get into. This day was no different. He had that same idiotic grin on his face and I knew that he was conjuring up something stupid in that small brain of his.

Mike wasn't the smartest guy in the world and he knew it. Even though he had a way of getting me into all kinds of trouble, my youthful instincts would always get the best of me. The fun we had outweighed all the common sense in the world.

"What's going on, man?" I asked, knowing that those tiny wheels in that head of his were cranking out formulas with all the wrong answers.

"Boy, I've got something that you won't believe," he replied with a look of incredible anxiety. He was so excited I thought that he would

Pit

burst. "I need you to meet me at the park 'round seven."

"Are you crazy? I have to be home by dark."

"Man, it don't git dark till nine; besides we'll be back way before then."

"So what's up?" I asked with a curious look.

"You'll see, man. Just meet me there and don't be late."

This wasn't like Mike. He usually would at least tell me whose window we were going to break or what tires we would flatten or what we would be stealing from the store around the corner. Just as quickly as he had come, he was gone. He didn't even ask to come in to play video games or ask for anything to eat. Not knowing what he was up to gave me mixed feelings. I was a little scared but overwhelmingly I was excited.

Pit

I got to the park about six. Mike hadn't arrived yet. I sat in the bleachers and watched some of the older guys play basketball. One of the guys had a boom box and a few of the rival break-dance groups were in their corner practicing for that weekend's break-dance contest in the park gym.

Soon it was six-thirty and there was Mike coming down the street. I got up and ran to meet him. On my way I noticed that Mike had someone with him that I had never seen before. He was much older than we were, at least fourteen. He had a bandana on his head and sneakers with no strings in them. He looked like a drug dealer and I wanted nothing to do with him.

"Here he is. This is my homeboy Larry," Mike said as I came up.

Pit

Mike had never referred to me as his "homeboy" before, so I figured this was his way of being cool.

"My name's Greg, but enough with the formalities, y'all goin' or not?"

"But where…."

Before I could finish my question, Mike interrupted, "Of course we're ready, man, come on."

Though I was feeling pretty reluctant, I went with them. We walked for about twenty minutes or so. Even though I was familiar with this part of the neighborhood, I had never walked this far away from home. This part of the neighborhood was well known for its drugs and slums. I was scared.

I knew that I couldn't show my fear because Mike and Greg would think that I was a punk. There was nothing worse than being thought of as soft or weak. If they had thought for a moment that I was scared, there would have been no way for me to recover from it. Who knew what Greg might do and Mike would never want to hang around with me again. Besides being afraid, my curiosity was getting the best of me too. Whatever was about to take place was not going to happen without me seeing it.

"H... h... how much further?" I asked in a scared, screeching voice.

"What the fuck wrong wit you, man? I know you ain't scared." Greg's voice was a lot deeper than ours and that was scary in itself. But still, I couldn't back down.

"No, I ain't scared; just ready to see what we walked all this way fo'."

We began to walk toward some heavily wooded areas of the neighborhood. The smell was almost unbearable and one that I would remember for the rest of my life. I

Pit

didn't know what it was, but I
realized later that it was the smell
of marijuana. But that wasn't all.
The smell of dead animal and smoke
also lingered in the air. In the
distance you could hear many voices,
as though we were going to some type
of sporting event.

As we got closer to the voices, I
noticed that we were coming to a
point where it seemed that the earth
stopped. We came to the edge of what
looked like a big hole in the earth.
It was like a big crater. It had to
be manmade, because it was a perfect
circle that formed a pit-like arena.

Around the arena were male
spectators drinking, smoking, and
using profane language, as though
they were at a world championship
wrestling match. The setting was like
a miniature stadium except, instead

of hotdogs and soft drinks sold from the local concession stand, drugs and wagering money circulated through the crowd. At the bottom of the arena was a dome-shaped cage with a small entrance on either end. It kind of reminded me of a small version of a lion tamer's cage at a circus.

Mike and I sat at the top so as not to draw too much attention to ourselves. Greg went down to be with some of the older men.

"So what do you think?" Mike had a look of excitement as though he had been here many times before.

"Just great, man," I responded with a little bitterness. I knew it was getting late and I couldn't just leave by myself.

"Just relax, man. This is going to be the most fun we have ever had."

Pit

I overheard the conversation of some of the other men. "I can't wait to see what ole Vicious does today."

"Oh yeah? Well, he better be ready 'cause Demon ain't no joke."

"One of these motherfuckers got a new bitch."

"Well, hope she ain't in heat. Shit, I ain't come to see no fuckin'. I come to see some fightin'."

Around the outside of the cage I could see men with barking dogs on chains. There were all types of mean and vicious looking dogs down there. Rottweilers, Doberman pinschers, and pit bulls were some of the most recognizable ones. Some were mixed breeds, half-Doberman half-German shepherd, and others just mutts. All of them had one thing in common. They were all killers.

Pit

Two owners brought the first two dogs into the cage. The owners held their dogs by their scruffs at the top of their necks. The two dogs snapped, barked and snarled at each other as the owners held them just close enough to smell each other.

The dog on the left was a brown pit bull with a patch of white around his right eye. Although he looked like a pretty young dog, he was very healthy and muscular looking. When he snarled and showed his teeth, he looked like he could kill a horse. I was sitting quite a way from the action but he struck a fear in me so deep that I was becoming short of breath.

The other dog was a Doberman with the standard black and brown Doberman colors. He was a beautiful dog but his rage made him look ugly. Why someone would subject a purebred

Pit

Doberman to this was beyond my understanding.

As a matter of fact, why would someone do this to any animal?

During the preliminaries, Mike gave me the play by play. "The reason why they hold 'em around the neck like that is to make 'em mean and ready to attack."

Mike barely knew the reason why the pencil had been invented, but I gave him the benefit of the doubt since he was more experienced in this field than I was.

Suddenly a whistle sounded and the owners let their dogs go. All the spectators were screaming and cheering.

"Get 'em, Vicious! Kill that mothafucka!" I heard one man scream.

Before I had a chance to wonder which one was Vicious, Mike enlightened me. "The pit bull is

Vicious. He's the toughest dog in the house. The Doberman is Demon."

The violent rage of both dogs was unbearable. Demon jumped out on top by getting behind Vicious and biting him in his left hip. It didn't take long for Vicious to recover and show me what Mike was talking about. Vicious was quick and strong, and with one fell swoop he jumped around and scratched Demon across the face with his paw. The next thing I knew, Vicious had one side of Demon's face locked in his jaws.

Demon was hurt but not done. He pulled away violently but he was seriously injured. Part of his face was hanging down and blood was pouring from his nose. The smell and sight of blood only made Vicious more determined to kill. He charged at Demon and locked his huge jaws around his neck. Demon let out a screeching

Pit

yell and a few seconds later Demon went down and stopped moving. As quickly as it started, it was over.

I could feel myself begin to get queasy and my stomach started to churn. But the drama wasn't over yet. Vicious' owner went into the pit and grabbed his dog by the scruff, took him from the cage, and locked him on his short chain to a tree far from everyone else. No "good dog" or "congratulations," just more mistreatment.

Demon looked pretty bad but he wasn't dead. Demon's owner was outraged. He went into the cage, pulled a .22 caliber pistol out from under his shirt and shot Demon in the back of the head. Blood and brains splattered up on the side of the cage.

My young body couldn't take it anymore. I ran to the top of the pit

Pit

and through the woods. I stopped at a tree and started throwing up. Mike ran behind me laughing and showing no pity for my condition.

"You can't handle it, man! You a punk?"

I was too sick to respond. After the last of my dinner came up, I began walking home at a fast pace. Mike was right behind me, laughing and teasing. I don't know if I was scared or angry. But I knew that I needed to get home before dark.

After Mike had had about as much fun as he could with me, he tried to slow me down. "Come on, man, stop walking so fast."

After calming down and catching my breath, I slowed down.

"Man, did you see that shit?" he said.

At first I didn't say anything. I just listened to him. As he talked, I

Pit

noticed that his voice kept getting higher pitched with each sentence.

His excitement grew and he spoke faster and faster as he went on and on about that dogfight. I began to realize that he was high. But we hadn't been close enough to the marijuana smokers for him to inhale contact smoke. No drug in the world could have given him this type of buzz.

He had gotten a big adrenaline rush from what he had just taken in and it would take him a while to come down off that high.

After a few more minutes of his rambling on, I interrupted him, "They didn't have to shoot 'em."

He stopped and gave me a look as though I was stupid for saying such a thing.

Pit

"What you mean, man? That's the rules: you lose you die, then they burn you."

He began to explain some of the other rules of this cruel sport. "Sometimes if your dog is real good, they put him up against two other dogs at once. If your dog wins, you become Lord of the Underground and you git much respect throughout the neighborhood."

"Oh yeah? Well, what do those dogs git?" I asked, shocked at what I was hearing.

"They git to live to fight another day. Man, they just dogs, besides most of 'em are stolen. The only good dog is a winnin' dog."

I couldn't believe what I was hearing. Here was the cold, hard truth about an insane sport. I knew that the drugs were illegal, but the dog fighting I wasn't too sure about.

Pit

However, my father once told me that if it didn't feel right, it probably wasn't.

I never went back to that place again, but Mike was an addict. His goal from then on was to become the best dog fighter ever and claim the title Lord of the Underground.

Finding My Friend

Pit

Time passed as time does and Mike and I grew apart. We still saw each other every now and then but we didn't hang out together anymore. The year was 1987 and it was another one of those lazy summers. This year I was able to work as a construction laborer with my uncle. The work was very strenuous, but the pay was pretty good. By the middle of the summer, I had earned a good bit of money and I knew exactly what I wanted to buy with it.

It had been a while since I had had my last puppy and I really wanted one. I had my eyes set on an English bulldog that I had seen in the mall pet shop. He was pretty expensive and I knew that I would have to save a little more money before I would be able to afford him. Not to mention, I still had to have money left over to

Pit

buy school clothes at the end of the summer.

One day my father came home from work and told me about someone who was selling a bulldog. He only wanted fifty dollars and the dog was healthy. The man and his family were about to move into an apartment that didn't allow pets. They really needed to get rid of the puppy.

I was very excited. This was well within my budget and I couldn't wait to go get him. My father and I decided we would go pick him up Saturday morning.

It seems that the more excited you get about something the longer it takes for it to happen. But Saturday morning finally arrived and we left early to get my new dog.

We drove for what seemed like forever until we reached a place deep in the country. We turned down a dirt

Pit

road and came to a trailer with a fence around it. We got out of the car, and as we approached the fence, the cutest little puppy came running out to greet us. He was nice, but he looked nothing like the dog in the mall. He had big floppy ears, and even though he had a few wrinkles in his face, they weren't well defined.

An old man walked out of the trailer and noticed my father right away. "Hey, Harry, how are you doing?"

"Fine, just fine," my father responded with a smile on his face.

"Come in through the fence."

The old man had more wrinkles in his face than the puppy and he looked old and tired.

"His name is Rambo," he said as he looked at me with his one good eye. "He's part English and part pit bull.

Pit

He was born Easter Sunday and he is three months old."

All I could think to myself was, *What kind of a name is that? How could you name him after a movie?* I was beginning to have second thoughts about this whole ordeal. I really wanted a purebred English bulldog and I wanted to name him myself.

Just when I was ready to call the whole thing off, Rambo came up to me and gave me a look that I just could not resist. I kneeled down to pet him and he responded by lying down and rolling over so that I could scratch his belly. He was a beautiful puppy with a gorgeous white coat and beautiful brown eyes. He looked up at me and gave me the sweetest whimper.

From then on I was hooked. A bond was formed between us that would never be broken. I paid the man his money and we took Rambo home.

Pit

After pulling into the driveway,
we got out and right away Rambo ran
around the yard as if he knew that he
was home. I wanted to change his name
but at three months old he responded
very well to Rambo. I tried to see if
he would catch on to a new name.

"Butch, come here!" I yelled as he
ran around the yard. But he just
ignored me and kept running.

When all else failed, I came to
realize, he would not respond to
anything else. It was settled. His
name was Rambo.

Although Rambo was playful, he was
very gentle and very affectionate.
For such a young puppy, he was very
smart. I taught him how to sit that
same day but he was too playful to
learn anything else. I began to
forget about all my disappointments
and love him just for being the dog
he was.

Pit

That night I put Rambo on our back porch to sleep. Our porch was closed in and carpeted, so I knew that it would be comfortable for him. I covered him up with a blanket and I left to go to bed.

No more than ten minutes passed before I began to hear the worst moaning and whimpering I had ever heard in my life. I put my pillow over my head to drown out the noise. After a while the shrill noise got louder and the pillow wasn't helping. It was late and the next day I had to get up early for Sunday school. In between the whining was barking, I could feel the anger building up inside me as he kept whining. Then it stopped.

I was so relieved. Finally I could turn over and get some sleep. No sooner than that thought entered my mind, he started up again. I couldn't

Pit

take it anymore. I stormed out of my bed and I was steaming mad. I slammed open the back porch door.

"What the hell are you…."

Before I could finish my words of anger, he looked up at me with those sad eyes and my anger turned to pity. I sat down, put him in my lap and began stroking the back of his coat. He was so happy to see me that he stood up and licked me all over my face.

After a while he got comfortable and I stood up to leave. As I began to walk through the door, he began to whine and moan again.

"Come on, boy, I gotta go to bed. I gotta get up early tomorrow."

But nothing I said made it any better. I knew that I couldn't leave him. I reached into one of the old storage cabinets where Mom kept my old toys and pulled out one of my old children's storybooks.

"Okay, you got me. This is one of my favorite stories. My mom use to read this to me when I couldn't sleep."

I sat down, put him in my lap, and began to read to him. "Once upon a time there were three bears who lived in a little cottage. There was the poppa bear, the momma bear and the baby bear."

Before I finished the book, Rambo was out cold. Since he was lying in my lap, I didn't want to move and take the chance of waking him up. I read a few more lines, and before I knew it, we were both fast asleep.

For a while, taking care of Rambo was pretty easy. But I found out that taking care of a puppy was a very tiring task, not to mention expensive. I had had a lot of puppies in the past but my father usually took care of the feeding and the shots and everything else that had to do with raising a dog. This time it was all on me.

My father had let me know before I bought Rambo that all of the burden would be on my shoulders. He would be there if I needed him but I had to take care of Rambo. My father was teaching me something that I would use for the rest of my life. It was called responsibility.

Since Rambo was still pretty young, my parents would sometimes let him sleep in the kitchen. Of course he had to be house broken and that task was not going to be easy. My father had to engineer this one, and then I learned from him.

"First of all, you have got to make sure that he has enough newspaper down for him to go on."

Pit

This one particular night, there was an incredible thunderstorm and it was raining unbelievably hard. Rambo had just finished eating and my mother asked my father to take him outside.

"But it's raining like hell out there! If he has to go, he can go right here on the floor."

By now my mother was pretty frustrated with my father. "If you start letting him shit on the floor now, you'll be sending him the wrong message and he may never learn the right way."

My father looked at my mother with a crazy frown on his face. "Look, if he shits on the floor, you can put my face in it and smack me across the nose with a rolled-up newspaper, 'cause I'll be damned if I'm going out in this thunderstorm to die!"

Pit

I guess my father's point was well taken, because after we had laughed at what he had just said, my mother pretty much left him alone.

Every day, before and after work, I walked Rambo, but my favorite thing was washing him.

Unlike most dogs, Rambo loved to be washed. He loved to be scrubbed, and that beautiful white coat of his shined when he was clean. Since he was white, I had to wash him often. I didn't mind because it was a very hot summer and the water helped us both stay cool.

After every wash, I would take him for a walk through the neighborhood. He was a natural show dog. He knew that he was a pretty dog and he flaunted it as though he knew all eyes were on him. Those who weren't afraid of him would come over and pet

Pit

him and ask questions about him. Most
of the men would ask if he were for
sale. No amount of money could
replace him. He was my best friend
and I was his.

The Promise

Pit

One day while walking him through the neighborhood we took a different route. I had been that way before but it had been a long time ago. We came to a house with a fence around it and Rambo was getting a little shaky.

As we got closer to the house, I could hear some snarling and growling. From the street I could see two big rottweilers going at each other's throats. I couldn't believe what I was seeing. I was so scared that I almost wet myself.

There was a man standing there watching as the two dogs went at it. A few seconds later, the man pulled them apart and put one of the dogs on a chain. The other dog must have smelled our presence because he charged toward the fence and barked and snarled at us. He looked as though he would kill us if he could get through that fence. My heart was

Pit

pumping so hard that it felt like it would burst through my chest and my blood pressure must have hit the roof.

I looked down at Rambo and I couldn't believe what he was doing. He looked as though he was taunting the ferocious beast. He put his nose up, walked around in a circle, and wagged his tail as though the snarling dog didn't concern him at all. In fact, I think he was enjoying himself.

The man walked up to the fence and noticed us right away. "That's a pretty dog. How much you want for him?"

I would have to be crazy to sell Rambo to this guy. "He's not for sale."

And with that, Rambo and I left for home. I felt really bad that

Pit

Rambo had to see what I considered cruelty.

I stopped, kneeled down and grabbed his head so that we were face to face. With a tear in the corner of my eye, I made him a promise.

"I swear that I'll never make you fight. I swear or may God strike me down. I love you more than anything in the world and I won't let anything happen to you."

As the tear rolled down my face, Rambo looked at me as though he were making a promise to me. He licked the tears from my face and looked at me as if to say, "Don't worry. I'll make sure nothing ever happens to you either."

After about three weeks of having Rambo, I felt that it was time to have his ears and tail clipped. It

Pit

seemed that everyone knew someone who could take care of this for me. I was told that I could even do it myself. All I had to do was take a rubber band and tie it around his tail. A few days later, his tail would just fall off. As for his ears, I could get one of the guys in the neighborhood to do it for a small fee. I heard that one guy used an axe to cut the ears.

My love for my dog made me afraid to try this without professional help. I called Rambo's vet and got all the information. I would have to take him in the morning and pick him up later on that afternoon. Rambo had been to the vet before for his shots but I had never had to leave him there. He would be given a sedative and everything would be done surgically. The whole procedure would cost ninety dollars.

Pit

The following morning my father and I took him to the vet. We arrived at the clinic around eight o'clock. Dr. Williams greeted us at the front of the vet clinic. She was a young lady in her late twenties or early thirties and she loved Rambo. She reached down to pet Rambo and he loved it.

"So how are you, boy? Have you been a good dog?"

If I didn't know any better, I would have thought that Rambo had a crush on her. She was always so polite to us.

"You can come pick him up at around three this afternoon," she told us.

I really don't think Rambo knew what he was in for, but I knew that he was in good hands. I felt comfortable knowing that Dr. Williams and Rambo got along well.

Pit

My father and I left and he dropped me off at my summer job. All day at work I could do nothing but think about Rambo and how good he would look once the procedure was over with.

After work my father and I went to pick Rambo up. We arrived at the vet clinic a little after three and Dr. Williams was waiting for us.

"The anesthetic hasn't worn off fully, so he'll be a little drowsy." She went to the back and brought him out.

He looked so funny. His tail had a bandage around it. Two Popsicle sticks wrapped with bandages held up both ears. He looked as if he had a football goalpost on top of his head. He was so drowsy that he could barely walk.

"The bandages will have to stay on for about a week. I put you down for an appointment on next Tuesday to have the bandages removed. Is this okay with you?"

"That's fine for us," my father replied. "Thanks for everything." With that we took Rambo home.

For the first couple of days, the bandages were very irritating to Rambo. He tried to take them off with his paws but his efforts were futile. Those bandages were there to stay. Just when he was starting to get used to them, it was time for them to be taken off.

The week passed and we took him to the vet that Tuesday afternoon. What seemed as though it would be an easy task was far from easy. The doctor had to use scissors to cut the bandages off and Rambo wanted no part of it. Dr. Williams finally brought the scissors out to the lobby and I had to hold Rambo down while she cut the bandages from his ears.

After she finally got the bandages off him, we were all exhausted, but it was worth it. He looked like a new dog. He had already been a good-looking dog but this made him look even better.

A few days passed and now that Rambo had a new look I was very anxious to show him off. We walked around to the neighborhood park. As soon as we arrived, everyone's attention was focused on us. There were other people with their dogs but theirs were of no comparison. I was so proud to have such a wonderful dog.

While in the park, I ran into Officer John Davis. He worked for the local police station and was always an organizer of all the park's activities. He was my flag football coach and a good friend to have.

"Hi, John! How is everything going?" I thought that it was cool of him to let us call him by his first name.

"Hey, Larry. Everything is fine. How come you aren't playing baseball this year?"

"I had to take this summer job and it takes up a lot of my time. I also have to take care of my dog."

He looked down at Rambo. "That's a nice looking dog you have there. He looks like you've been taking good care of him."

"He is a big responsibility but I love it."

I was very proud of Rambo and John could tell. John and I said our goodbyes and I headed for home. Rambo was indeed a very handsome dog. But it wouldn't be long before I learned

Pit

that his looks weren't the only thing
special about him.

Pit

My Savior

Pit

One day after work while sitting at home playing video games, my mom asked me to go to the store for her. My father would be home soon and he wanted to show Rambo off to a couple of his friends. So instead of taking Rambo with me, I rode my bike. On the way back from the store, I rode at a pretty slow pace.

I was just up the street from my house when I looked over my shoulder and noticed that there was a guy about one hundred yards away walking two dogs. One of the dogs looked like a puppy rottweiler and the other was a full-grown pit bull. I turned around and continued my ride home. A few seconds later I began to hear growling behind me. I turned around again and the pit bull had gotten loose and was in a full charge toward me.

Pit

My heart began to race and sweat poured from my face as my fear reached a level that I hadn't felt in a long time. I began to pedal as fast as I could but the dog kept gaining on me. It felt like everything was happening in slow motion. The way that dog was snarling I knew that if he caught me I was a goner. I kept pedaling as fast as I could. I looked down and saw a small bump in the road. I did everything I could to avoid it but I couldn't.

My front wheel hit the bump. I tried to maintain control of the bike but the crash was too violent. The bike jerked and I flew over the handlebars. I landed, scraping my hands and knees on the pavement, but I was far from being out of danger. The dog was charging at me in a violent rage, when out of nowhere a

Pit

streak of white flashed in front of me.

I looked up and there was Rambo fighting off this dog. The two dogs separated and stood there staring each other down.

"Damian, sit!"

As soon as this dog heard his master, he stopped and sat there in front of Rambo. I was still scared from the ordeal but I couldn't help feeling amazed at the obedience of this seemingly vicious animal. The owner and his puppy got to his dog and he put the leash back on him. I quickly grabbed Rambo by his collar.

When I looked up at the owner, I couldn't believe my eyes. It was Mike and he had this crazy look on his face. This was the first time I had seen him in a while and he had changed a lot since our younger days. Like mine his skin was dark, but he had a very muscular build. He looked as though he worked out with the Incredible Hulk.

By now Mike was into all kinds of mischief. Drug dealing and theft were just two. His biggest thing was dog fighting. He had also become one of the neighborhood bullies. He had a lot of boys my age and younger scared of him. He did the typical bully stuff—taking lunch money, teasing and harassing people.

I don't know if it was knowing him from my childhood days or if it was knowing how incredibly ignorant he was that made me so unafraid of him. To me he was just another punk and I had no reason to fear him. That was until this day.

"That's a healthy mutt you got there. He looks like he could hold his own. How much you want for 'em?"

Pit

I got up and noticed the bruises on my hands and legs. But Mike wasn't concerned about my well-being.

"He's not for sale!" I responded angrily.

"That's too bad. That mothafucka need to be in the pit. That's where you can find out how good a dog he really is. You better be glad I got here when I did or Damian would have fucked his ass up."

I was too scared to respond to anything he was saying. I looked Damian over and saw he was a reddish-brown color with a red nose. He looked about two years old.

"This puppy is one of my newest additions." I looked down at his puppy as he spoke of her. "Her name is Joan of Ark and she gonna be the baddest bitch in the pit."

She was a pretty puppy and someone would have to be pretty crazy to put her in the pit. I was convinced that Mike was definitely that someone.

"Well, Larry, I guess I'll see you around." And with that he left.

For some reason I was totally convinced that this would not be my last run-in with Mike. To this day I can never be sure if Damian actually got loose by accident or if Mike turned him loose on me. Nevertheless I was grateful to Rambo. He may have saved my life and I felt that I owed my life to him. He was truly a special dog.

Pretty soon it was time to go back to school. I had had a very good summer and I couldn't wait to share it with my friends.

For some reason this school year was filled with rumors of how the pit bull was one of the most vicious dogs to own. Every other day, it seemed

Pit

that the news had something on
television about pit bulls attacking
people. It was even reported that
some dogs would attack their owners.

I didn't want to believe it but
there it was on television and in the
newspapers. I loved Rambo but all
this talk about dog attacks made me
pretty nervous. I started to question
my relationship with Rambo. And even
though I didn't want to admit it, I
was beginning to get scared. Would he
ever attack me? I'd only seen him
show aggressive behavior once and
that was when he was saving my life.

One evening, I watched in horror
as the evening news ran a story about
a recent dog attack.

"In today's news a five-year-old
girl was attacked by a pit bull. For
a full report we'll go to Joe
Anderson who is live on the scene.

Pit

"Thanks Dan. We're here at Johnson County Hospital in the small town of Thomas, Georgia, where a little girl was brought in after a brutal attack by the new family watchdog. Apparently the father of the little girl brought a stray dog home after work to keep as a pet. This afternoon Mrs. Walker took her daughter out in the backyard to play with their new dog. Everything seemed to be going well when the unthinkable happened. We are with the mother of the little girl, who is anxiously waiting for an update from the doctor."

This was unbelievable. I looked on as the news reporter asked the mother to give her account of what happened.

Pit

"Miss Walker, I know that this has been a very tough ordeal, but can you tell us what happened?"

"Two days ago my husband brought this dog home to keep as a watchdog. He works a lot, so he figured we could use the dog for protection. I wanted to make a home video of Sarah playing with her new pet. I took Sarah out to play with this dog and at first I was nervous about having her around a strange dog. After a while I was relieved because the dog was so friendly and playful. I turned around to set up my tripod for my video camera and I heard my baby start screaming."

By now the mother was starting to get upset. She started crying as she kept telling the world about her gruesome ordeal. As she kept telling the story, they played her video. The dog was a jet-black color. His ear and tail hadn't been clipped, so he looked fairly young. He seemed to be as playful as a new puppy from the pet shop. She continued on as the video rolled.

"With no warning at all, the dog jumped on my baby and began biting her on her face and stomach. I screamed at the top of my lungs. GET OFF OF MY BABY!!! SOMEBODY HELP ME!!! Somehow he locked his jaws like a vice grip around her arm and would not let go. My baby was crying so hard that I thought she would die. I took off my shoe and tried to beat him off of her but it didn't work."

I couldn't believe it. Out of nowhere this seemingly playful dog just started attacking this innocent little girl. The violent rage of this dog made me wonder if the same would happen to me. This was almost too much for me to handle. I sat up in my seat shocked at what she was saying and what I was seeing. This dog was relentless in his attack.

"Out of nowhere, my next-door neighbor, Jack, appeared with a baseball bat. He swung, hitting the dog in the back of the head. It took about three licks before the dog finally let go. Jack grabbed Sarah and we all ran into the house."

In the middle of the report they flashed to a video of the dog being taken out of the backyard by the police and animal control. He looked like a pit bull mixed with a German Shepard. I couldn't say for sure what he was mixed with. I could see how the father could have made the mistake of bringing him home. He seemed very docile and was very playful as he was being escorted from the backyard. I guess you really never know with stray dogs.

The camera swung around showing the doctor emerging from the emergency room. It didn't take long before reporters and TV cameras surrounded the doctor.

"Doctor, can you tell us the condition of little Sarah?"

"She has suffered major damage to her left eye. It's a fifty-fifty chance that she will lose some if not all sight in that eye. She received multiple cuts and bruises in the abdomen area and a five-inch long laceration on her left arm. Her arm will require about 50 to 60 stitches. It's going to be a long, painful recovery."

After the doctor's, report I was sick. How could something like this happen to such a young little girl? Just then they flashed to another reporter, who had a dog expert on the scene.

"Dr. King, what causes a seemingly docile animal to commit such a hideous act?"

With a sigh and small gesture, the doctor replied.

"Some of these dogs are trained to attack. This breed of dog in particular can be trained to attack when they hear a certain code word or if they see someone make some sort of small gesture. It could be the raising of an arm, a facial expression, or anything that could set these animals off. Sarah must have done or said something to trigger this reaction."

They then flashed to the dog pound. There in the cage sat the pit bull with, what seemed, an expression of confusion.

"Why these dogs attack, no one can be sure. Unfortunately this little fellow will be put to sleep. This is Joe Anderson reporting for WLTX channel 19 news."

While I was watching the dog attack story on the news, my mother came into the den and sat down next to me. She could tell that something was wrong with me.

Pit

Before she could inquire into my situation, I asked her the big question.

"Momma, do you think Rambo would ever attack me?"

She paused a second. "Son, you have to realize that those dogs are trained to be aggressive and they receive a lot of abuse. There is a saying that goes, 'Never bite the hand that feeds you.' I believe that if this same hand is abusive towards you, eventually you will retaliate. But if this hand shows you love and respect, then you will give that same love and respect in return. You and Rambo have love and respect between you."

I was convinced that Rambo was special and I was upset with myself for thinking otherwise. I wanted to change the minds of my friends, so I wrote a term paper on the subject.

Pit

I found out some very interesting things about pit bulls while doing my research. For instance I had no idea that these dogs played important acting and advertisement roles. Pete, the dog that stared in the *Little Rascals,* was a pit bull. The dog on one of my favorite snacks, Cracker Jacks, was also a pit bull.

I'm not sure where the name "pit bull" originated from, but in dog shows they are referred to as the Staffordshire bull terrier. They were originally bred in England around the 1800s for a sport called "pit rat killing." Later they were used for dog fighting before the sport was banned in England. Known for their loyalty and calmness toward humans, these dogs were now well respected among show dogs and had won many awards.

Pit

Although I received an "A" for my efforts, I don't think I was successful in changing anybody's mind about pit bulls.

Finding Him A Mate

Pit

As the school year pressed on, spring began to fill the air. A new season was upon us, and the nice weather and warmer temperatures were a welcome sight. Flowers were beginning to bloom and the chirping of the birds got louder every day. It was almost Easter--Rambo's birthday—and I wanted to do something special for him.

The Saturday before Easter Sunday, I bought him a chewable dog bone with a ribbon wrapped around it. I put one of those paper party hats on his head and sang "Happy Birthday" to him. I took him to the front yard and some of the neighborhood kids, who were playing in the street, noticed Rambo wearing the birthday hat.

"Ooh, is it Rambo's birthday?"

You would think that the birthday hat would have given them a clue, but kids can still ask dumb questions.

Pit

Before I could even answer, some of them, at least those who weren't afraid of him, came over to pet him and wish him a happy birthday. It wasn't long before we were all singing "Happy Birthday" to Rambo again.

It was just then when Rambo decided that he wanted to give me a present of his own. He jumped on my leg and began to hump away as though there was no tomorrow. The kids thought that this was the funniest thing and fell on the ground laughing. I was so embarrassed. Rambo didn't care; he just kept on going like the Energizer Bunny. It took all of my strength to pry him off me.

After a while it started to get embarrassing to play with Rambo in public. It seemed that one of my legs was more important to him than anything else. No matter what time of

Pit

day or where we might be, he had no problem showing his never-ending affection for my leg. It didn't take a rocket scientist to figure out that it was time to find him a mate. I didn't want to mate him with just any dog though.

Although I had gotten many offers to stud Rambo, I wanted to be sure that the other owner was responsible. After some looking around, I finally went to my father for help. Before I could ask, my dad was already on top of the situation.

"Son, there is someone who has a nice-looking female pit bull for Rambo to mate with."

"What does she look like?" I asked very anxiously.

"She is very healthy and she is ready for a mate too. I noticed how friendly Rambo has been to you lately

Pit

and figured it was about that time."
He had a silly grin on his face.

"That's very funny, Dad, but I've
seen the way he looks at your legs
too."

"We'll take him tomorrow
afternoon," he said.

"Thanks, Dad."

After school the next day, my dad
and I loaded Rambo in the car and
took him to meet his Juliet. We
arrived and pulled into the driveway
of a large, red-bricked house with a
fence around it. We unloaded Rambo,
and right away I noticed him getting
excited. He had his nose in the air,
as though he could smell a good meal.

"He can smell that bitch in heat,"
a voice from inside the fence said.

A man about my father's age came
out of the fence. "So this is the

Pit

handsome dog you've been telling me about."

"Yeah, he's the one," my father responded. "Hey, Jerry, this is my son, Larry, and his dog, Rambo."

I didn't ask, but my guess was this was someone my father worked with. I shook his hand but I was anxious to see this female that was getting Rambo so excited. He hadn't even seen her yet, but I could tell he was more than ready to go to work.

"My dog's name is Diamond. She's a year old and never mated before. I only hope she is ready to meet your dog."

Rambo was getting restless, and if it hadn't been for his choke chain, I probably wouldn't have been able to control him.

My father looked down at him with a grin on his face. "Women have a way of doing that to you."

Pit

After a while Diamond came up to the fence where we could see her. She was a beautiful black and white pit bull with a muscular build. Rambo ran up to the fence and they both began to sniff each other as though this was a formal greeting. They didn't seem to show any negative aggression toward each other, so I figured it was safe to let Rambo inside the fence.

"Mr. Jerry, do you think it's all right to let them be together?"

"There's only one way to find out."

As he opened the gate, I took Rambo off his leash and he and Diamond ran to the backyard.

"I guess he'll be okay here for a few days," my father said as we began to make our way to the car.

Pit

I didn't even get to say goodbye. This was the first time Rambo would be away from home. I think that I was the furthest thing from his mind right then. I didn't mind though, because I knew that this was what he needed. Besides I would come by every day after school.

Before we got into the car, my father looked the situation over. "I guess we can leave him here for about a week."

A nod from Mr. Jerry was the only response, and with that, we were off.

Every day after school I would go to see how Rambo and his new mate were getting along. After a couple of days, Mr. Jerry and I became pretty good friends and we talked quite a bit. Even though Rambo was Diamond's first mate, this was not Mr. Jerry's first experience with breeding dogs. It was pretty nice, because I could

Pit

talk to Mr. Jerry about things that I couldn't necessarily talk about with other adults.

"So why did you want to start breeding dogs anyway?"

He looked at me as though he really didn't want to answer that question. "Well, at first it was for the money, but later it just got kind of fun. At one point I was breeding them to fight them, but decided after a while it was time to give that up when I had a bad experience with one of my dogs. Now I won't even think of selling one to anybody who is thinking of fighting them."

That was a huge relief because I wanted no part of that either.

"Besides fighting them, why do people love owning these dogs so much?"

Mr. Jerry smiled as though he couldn't wait to share his philosophy on the matter. "I think one word could sum it all up for you—power. I like to call them muscle dogs, which can be an extension of the young male ego. Like a weapon, these dogs can be a great equalizer for someone who is otherwise weak and afraid. These pit bulls, as well as your rottweilers, Doberman pinschers and even German shepherds, can be just as dangerous as a loaded gun when in the wrong hands. Sometimes when young men such as yourself get their hands on such animals, the power is very overwhelming."

I had to admit it. Sometimes when I walked Rambo, I really had no fear of anyone. In fact some people would cross the street before they would get to us. It really made me feel invincible.

I really liked coming over to talk to Mr. Jerry. He was a pretty nice

Pit

man. I especially liked it when his wife would bake cookies for me. Mr. Jerry's wife was a very pretty lady named Sharon. I called her Miss Sharon out of respect. She didn't speak much, but when she did she always had a kind word.

Proud Papa

Pit

After some time I was beginning to wonder if Rambo and Diamond were ever going to be done with their breeding episodes. It was kind of embarrassing watching those two go at it all out in the open with not a care in the world. But somehow Mr. Jerry knew when it was time for Rambo to go home.

After about two to three weeks, Diamond began to show signs of pregnancy. Her belly was a little bigger and little nipples began to show on her stomach. After some time I noticed that she was starting to get a little irritable and getting too close to her wasn't a very good idea. It was time to leave her alone for a while. So Rambo and I did.

For a few weeks Rambo and I stayed away from Mr. Jerry's house, to let nature take its course. We spent a lot of time in the park and just taking walks through the neighborhood.

About eight weeks passed before I decided it was time to go check on Rambo's little woman. We arrived at Mr. Jerry's and he was very excited to see us as he came to open the fence to the backyard.

"Come on in, you two," he said as we walked past the open gate. He kneeled down to stroke Rambo's fur. "You should be quite proud of yourself."

"So how's Diamond doing?" I couldn't wait to hear the news and Mr. Jerry could tell too.

"She is doing wonderful. And so are the puppies."

"*Puppies!*"

I don't know why I was surprised. I mean that was why we had come in the first place. I guess the thrill of having puppies around made any young child excited.

"How many?" I asked with an unbearable anxiety. I don't even think I wanted to hear the answer. I wanted to see the answer for myself.

Without saying another word Mr. Jerry escorted us to the backyard. There for the first time I saw them. Diamond was lying on her side while the cutest litter of six puppies suckled their mother's nipples and let out the sweetest little whimpers.

"They are one week old today," Mr. Jerry whispered as Rambo and I looked on in awe. "There are four girls and two boys."

I could see that Mr. Jerry had already made quite a few observations. After a few moments, I was able to make a few of my own. Two of the puppies looked exactly like their mother with the same black and white color pattern. One puppy, who was the runt of the bunch, was white with tiny black spots and looked just like her father. The other three puppies were also black and white but had a different pattern than their mother.

I wanted to take Rambo closer but Diamond was not ready for that at all. She growled and snarled at my advance, and there was no way I was going to mess with a very protective mother.

Mr. Jerry was quick to warn me. "I don't think she's ready for anyone to be close to her puppies yet. I'm the only one that she will tolerate right now. Give it a couple of weeks."

This was definitely a very exciting time for Rambo and me. I had seen plenty of puppies but never

Pit

before they had been weaned from their mother.

Every day after school I would walk Rambo through the neighborhood and end up at Mr. Jerry's house. Every day was pretty much routine, except for one particular day. By now most of the neighborhood knew about the newborn puppies and pit bulls were the dog of choice. On this day while walking toward the park, I ran into none other than Mike himself.

I had seen him around but we never talked to each other. I didn't like being around him because you never knew what he might do. To most of the kids in the 'hood, he was a bully. After our earlier run-in, I had managed to keep him at a safe distance until this day.

As he approached me, Rambo began to bark violently at him. With my right hand still in the leather loop of his leash, I grabbed the chain links with my left and pulled back on his chain. "No, Rambo, sit."

Lord knows I wanted to let that chain go, but for some reason I was kind of curious to see what he wanted.

"You know, if I had one of my dogs here, your boy wouldn't have a chance."

Rambo was still barking and with every one of Mike's steps I would let one link of the chain slip through my fingers. "Why don't you calm him down, man? I just wanted to holla at you for a minute."

I could tell he was starting to get a little scared. I guess this was that power that Mr. Jerry had been talking about. I wanted to let that chain go but I think I was more interested in what he had to say than

Pit

letting Rambo rip his head off. It was obviously something important since it had been a while since he had approached me. I grabbed Rambo by the collar to restrain him but Mike knew not to come too close.

"What's up, big Larry? Haven't seen you around in a while."

His bloodshot eyes and slurring voice told me that he had either been drinking or smoking something. The "big Larry" thing made me even more suspicious since he had never called me that before.

"What's up with you?" I tried to use the toughest masculine tone I could muster from my changing voice.

"I hear your dog there made some puppies with Mr. J's dog. What a brother gotta do to get one? I just lost one of my best dogs in a fight a couple of days ago. I only had 'em for a week. You should have seen it.

Pit

I put Buster in the pit with two
other dogs, a rottweiler and some
mutt. Buster came out on the attack."

He had to know that I didn't want
to hear this. He just kept going on
and on anyway. He acted as if we were
still the best of friends.

"He went after that mutt like a
fly to shit. The mutt did okay for a
while but he didn't last long. Buster
was too fuckin' fast for his ass. He
locked them big jaws around that
mutt's neck and he was done for. You
could hear the neck crack from a
block away, as Buster clamped down on
him. The rottweiler was a whole
different story. They started off toe
to toe with both dogs going for each
other's throats. The next thing I
knew the rottweiler was on top of
Buster. That rottweiler grabbed
Buster's neck and ripped it wide

open. Blood and shit splashed all over the place. That shit was wild!"

Mike had the biggest grin on his face. He didn't even care that his own dog was just killed. He had no remorse at all. All he cared about was a good fight.

I paused for a second to get my thoughts together.

"Those pups aren't for sale to fighters."

He had a shocked look on his face. "What the hell you mean, man? Mr. J is the...." He stopped midway through his sentence and began to chuckle a little. "Never mind, man. I'll talk to Mr. J myself." And with a smart aleck gesture and smirk on his face, he ran off.

Later that afternoon, I walked Rambo over to Mr. Jerry's house to check on the new family. By now the

Pit

puppies were a little older with their eyes open. Though they were still not weaned from their mother yet, they had become a little more active. Diamond was a lot more receptive and a little less protective. Yet I stayed clear anyway and let Mr. Jerry do the handling of the puppies.

All six puppies were healthy according to the vet. Even the runt was starting to catch up in size with her siblings. I also noticed that she had a lot more spunk than the others. She was the first one of the litter that Mr. Jerry brought over to me to hold. I fell in love with her at first sight. According to our secret agreement, I would get one female puppy and I knew right away that she would be it.

While playing with the pup, I began to tell Mr. Jerry about my run-

in with Mike earlier that day. "Mr.
Jerry, today I saw one of the guys in
the neighborhood that is definitely a
dog fighter."

I didn't feel comfortable telling
an adult about one of the kids in the
neighborhood, but I knew that if I
didn't, he might make the fatal
mistake of selling one of the puppies
right into the fighting pit and
eventually to its death. I didn't
dare tell him about the drug dealing.

"You're talking about Mike. He was
here about an hour before you got
here. We got into a little argument
because I refused to sell him a
puppy. I know about all the shit he's
into and he knew that I wouldn't dare
do business with him."

I was relieved that I didn't have
to tell him everything about Mike. I
was also happy to hear Mr. Jerry
stand by his word. It was starting to

Pit

get late, so Rambo and I said our
goodbyes and left for home.

Total Chaos

Pit

The next day I awoke to a dreary Saturday morning. It was cloudy out but it wasn't raining. But, hey, at least it was the weekend. The weekend meant two things: no school, and more time to spend with Rambo and his new family.

I got up out of bed, washed up, and went out to greet Rambo. It was as if he knew that the rest of the day was ours.

"You ready to go for a walk today, boy?"

He jumped up at me and licked my face as I tried to put his leash on his collar. We had got about a block away from Mr. Jerry's house when I began to get an eerie feeling. I didn't know why, but I felt that something was wrong. We were outside of Mr. Jerry's house when I called for him to let us in the gate.

Pit

Mr. Jerry's wife Sharon came running to the gate. She had a very disturbed look on her face.

"Larry, I don't know how to tell you this, so I'll let you see it for yourself."

I walked through the gate to the backyard to find total chaos. All the puppies had been maimed to death. Most of them were unrecognizable and the smell was horrible. Diamond lay in a hole that had to have just been dug by Mr. Jerry. She was bloody all over and her frail body looked as though she was asleep, but I knew better.

In the far corner of the yard lay a brownish, red-nosed pit bull. I knew right away whom the dog belonged to. It was Mike's dog Damian. Miss Sharon walked up to me and put her hand on my shoulder. I think I may

Pit

have been in too much shock and disbelief to cry.

"This dog somehow got into the fence last night and attacked and killed Diamond and the puppies. Jerry had to shoot him."

Miss Sharon had a look of despair and disbelief as though she had been through a terrible ordeal. She was distraught and her hands shook nervously as she spoke. She began to tell me about what had transpired the night before.

"I was awakened last night to loud growls and snarls. I knew right away that something was wrong with the dogs. I ran downstairs to the back door and cut on the outside light. There I saw Diamond in an attack position with that brown pit bull facing her growling. She was ready to defend her puppies at all costs. I yelled to Jerry to get his gun.

Pit

"Diamond jumped out at the strange dog and attacked right away. But this dog was relentless in his attack and would stop at nothing to get to Diamond and her puppies. Diamond had locked her jaws around his hind leg but the other dog was too fast and too strong for her. Before I knew it, she was on her back and the dog locked his jaws around her neck and strangled her to death.

"Then he began to attack each puppy as they started to whine and cry out as if they knew they had just lost their mother. One by one he locked those massive jaws around each puppy and violently shook their heads until they were dead. He got to the last puppy, but before he could get a good grip on it, Jerry fired. The big dog released the puppy and fell dead on the ground," she said finishing her gruesome story.

Pit

As I stood there and stared at the carnage that lay in front of me, I felt a tear begin to swell in the corner of my eye. It was hard to imagine that someone would go to those great lengths to hurt innocent puppies and their mother. The evil within the hearts of some men could tear a whole world apart.

Right then, as fate would have it, a light drizzle began to fall. And just then it occurred to me—one of the puppies was still alive! I turned to Miss Sharon, but before I could ask, she answered my question.

"Jerry took the only surviving puppy to the vet first thing this morning."

But which puppy survived the ordeal? As Miss Sharon began to ramble on about the situation, I only heard bits and pieces of information.

Pit

The most important thing was that the puppy had been taken to the same vet that I took Rambo to.

In mid-sentence I stopped her, and apologized. "I'm sorry, Miss Sharon, but I have to hurry home."

I grabbed Rambo and made my way home as fast as I could. I got to my front yard and saw my dad standing in the driveway.

"Boy, what are you doing outside in this rain?"

Before he could really begin to lay into me, he realized that something was very wrong with me. "Son, what's wrong with you?"

At that point I couldn't hold it in any longer. I broke down and started crying. My dad grabbed Rambo and took him to the backyard. I walked with him and began to tell him the whole story.

Pit

"Are you sure it's the same vet that we take Rambo to?"

Once he was convinced that it was the same vet, we got into the car and raced over.

We walked into the lobby of the vet clinic to find Mr. Jerry sitting there with a bewildered look on his face. He stood up as my father and I walked over to him.

"I guess y'all seen what happened, huh?"

My father shook his head. "Yeah, Larry told me all about it. So how's the puppy doing?"

"The doc has her in the back. They've been back there for a while. Out of all those puppies, it was the little runt that survived."

Dr. Williams walked into the lobby. "Hi, Larry, how are you doing? What brings you by?"

Pit

Mr. Jerry answered for me. "His dog is the father of that puppy you have back there. So how's she doing?"

Dr. Williams gave a short pause. "She's doing well now but I will have to keep her here overnight before letting her go home."

I felt a little relieved, but Mr. Jerry gave a response that I couldn't believe. "If she's going to be too much trouble, you can put her to sleep."

I looked at my father with a look of great disappointment. "No, we can't let her be put to sleep! Let me have her. I'll take care of her. Please…."

"Son, you know we can't afford to have two dogs. Rambo is already a handful."

Mr. Jerry looked at my father. "If you want her, you can have her."

Pit

Frustrated with his loss, Mr. Jerry left.

I continued to make my plea. "Dad, I will take a job after school if I have to. Please let me take care of her. Once she gets well enough we can give her away."

I don't think I realized what I was saying at the time, but it worked.

My dad asked the doctor a few questions. "What exactly would we have to do to take care of her?"

Dr. Williams began to run off a laundry list. "First of all, she hasn't been weaned from her mother yet, so you will have to feed her baby formula for a couple of weeks. That means you have to buy baby bottles. I'll just make a list and have it ready for you when you come back to pick her up tomorrow."

Pit

My dad looked at me. "Okay, son, I'll let you do this but don't think this is going to be easy. Dr. Williams, can we see her?"

"Sure, follow me."

We followed her to the back. I was a little excited, not just because I was going to see my new little friend, but because this was the first time I would be going through those doors to the back. We walked down the hall and all I could hear were dogs barking. I looked in one room and noticed one of the nurses giving a dog a shot.

We got to the puppy's room and I saw her lying there on the table covered with bandages. She was weak and I knew that it would take a lot to get her up and about again. She had her father's pretty brown eyes and white spotted coat. She gave out a small whimper as I approached the table.

"Can I touch her?" I asked, feeling a little afraid that I would hurt her more.

"Sure, go ahead. You're going to be her primary caregiver from now on, so she's going to have to get used to you."

I began to stroke the top of her head and she seemed to relax with every stroke. I was already in love with her—I had been from the first time we had met. Right then and there, I knew that I would have to be her protector. I was determined to make sure that she regained her strength and I couldn't wait to get her home. My father and I left the vet and went home to prepare for the new puppy's arrival.

Pit

Nursing Her Back to Health

Pit

My parents decided that it would be best for me to keep her in the house until she regained her strength. I had a big box with a blanket and a pillow set out for her arrival. My mother was very instrumental in helping me prepare the puppy's new home. She gave me instructions on preparing the bottles of baby milk, as well as on taking care of her day-to-day needs.

The next day we went to church as we did every Sunday and I remember saying a little prayer to myself. *Dear God, please watch over my new little friend. She is very fragile and really needs you to watch over her. I would give anything to see her grow into a beautiful dog. In the name of Jesus, amen.*

It was in church that day that her name came to me. I would call her "Heaven." After a long day in church,

Pit

it was finally time for us to go get
my little friend. We arrived at the
vet at around three that afternoon
and Dr. Williams was waiting for us.

"She's doing better today, but
only you can make the difference in
whether she makes it or not. Have you
come up with a name for her yet?"

I smiled at her. "Yes, her name
will be Heaven. I came up with that
name in church today."

"That's a fine name, Larry."

With that she went to get Heaven
from the back. She still looked
pretty fragile but a little more
active than the day before. Dr.
Williams helped us put her in the car
and we took her home.

The first day having Heaven home
was a nightmare. I had forgotten how
a little puppy like Heaven could be
so much hell. My mother helped me
make her bottles of baby milk and

Pit

left pretty much everything else to me.

"Are you hungry, little lady?"

She seemed so helpless, but no matter what, I was going to be there for her. I sat down, put her in my lap, and began to feed her. It was like she hadn't eaten for days. I finished feeding her and put her in the box. As soon as I turned to walk away, she began to whine and cry as if someone was killing her. My first thought was, *Not again.* Her father had been bad enough.

I grabbed her out of the box and sat on the floor, cradling her like a little baby. I rocked her and sang lullabies until she fell asleep. My mother walked in and noticed that she was asleep. She looked at me as though I had just committed the biggest crime.

Pit

"What are you doing? Are you crazy?"

Now I was deeply confused. I had put her to sleep so she wouldn't make any noise and now I was getting yelled at for it.

"It is too early for her to be sleeping. If she sleeps now, she'll be up all night. Wake her up right now."

After all that hard work to get her to sleep I had to wake her up. Just then I started to remember my not-so-pleasant experiences with Rambo when I first brought him home. My mother was right, and though Heaven cried the rest of the afternoon, she did sleep through the night.

A couple of days passed and Heaven seemed to be doing a lot better. Even though I thought it was too early to let Rambo play around her, I would let him sit on the back porch next to the kitchen door while I fed her. Sometimes I would open the door slightly and let him look in at his baby girl. Most of the time, it didn't seem that he was concerned with her, but I still felt that someday they would have to form some kind of a bond.

One morning I got up and went into the kitchen to check on Heaven. I looked down and noticed that even though she was conscious she wasn't moving. I didn't dare pick her up; instead I stroked her fur.

"What's wrong, girl?"

As I stroked her fur she let out a little moan and I knew that something was very wrong. I ran to my parents' room and woke my father.

"Dad, Dad, there's something wrong with Heaven!"

Pit

My dad and mom woke and noticed the worried look on my face.

"What's wrong with her?" they both asked almost simultaneously.

"She's not moving!"

My father sprang from the bed and ran into the kitchen with me right behind him. He looked inside the box and noticed her fragile condition.

"We've got to get her to the vet."

Very rarely do I see my father panic, but this time he was close to it. Seeing him like that only scared me more.

"Larry, help me get her to the car."

We picked her up and moved her as carefully as possible outside and into the car. My father drove as fast as he could to Dr. Williams' office. Lucky for us she was just opening up and we went right on in. Dr. Williams

Pit

had noticed our looks of urgency and knew that something was wrong.

"Dr. Williams, it's Heaven. We woke up this morning to find her not looking too well. She's out in the car."

She grabbed her stethoscope and ran out to the car with us. As Dr. Williams looked her over. I couldn't help but feel that this couldn't be happening. For the few days that I had had her home she seemed to be doing well.

Dr. Williams looked up. "Okay, help me get her inside."

She and my father gently lifted her from the backseat and took her into the office doors and straight to the back. They put her up on the table where the doctor began to probe a little more. She looked at my father.

Pit

"I'm going to have to run some tests on her and I'll give you a call later this afternoon."

I wanted so much to stay with her but I knew that there was nothing more I could do. With a worried look on both our faces, my father and I left for home.

On the way home, my father knew that I was upset. "Son, I know this is difficult, but no matter what happens, you did the best you could. I'm proud of you, son."

No words could console me that day. We got home and I went to the only friend that I felt I could talk to in this situation. Rambo was sitting there in the yard oblivious of what was going on. It always seemed that he could tell when something was wrong with me. As I walked up to greet him, he jumped up

Pit

and licked me all over my face. This was a little more affection than I usually got but I loved every minute of it. I calmed him down, knelt on one knee and began to tell him about Heaven.

"We had to take Heaven to the vet. She's not doing too well, boy. We have to hope and pray that she pulls through."

I couldn't hold back any more. The tears welled up and pretty soon they flooded my face. I hugged Rambo around his neck and he licked my face as if he somehow knew that everything would be all right.

Later that afternoon, Dr. Williams called my father. I stood next to him as she gave him all the information. I was getting very anxious because all I could hear was a lot of "yeah, a huh" from my father. He hung up the phone and began to tell me everything.

"She's got a touch of pneumonia. They're not sure if she's going to make it. The doctor gave her some antibiotics and they are going to keep her for a couple of days. She'll call us back in a few days to let us know how she's doing. All we can do now is wait."

That three days' wait was almost unbearable. In those three days, I think I must have said a million prayers. Rambo and I would take walks and I would always have her on my mind.

Finally the third day came. After I got back from walking Rambo, my father ran up to me and, with a look of excitement. He urged me to hurry and put Rambo in the backyard so we could go.

Pit

"The vet just called and she wants to see us right away."

We rushed to the vet and went into the lobby where Dr. Williams was waiting for us. She didn't hesitate.

"You guys, follow me to the back."

We got to the back and I was amazed at the sight. There she was, little Heaven running around on the floor with the bandages off. I hadn't seen her with this much spunk since before the attack.

"She looks great. What did you do?" I asked with a great deal of disbelief.

"Well, Larry, she responded to the antibiotics we gave her and came through like a champ."

Like a champ was right. I guess all that praying had paid off. My dad and I were so happy we couldn't thank Dr. Williams enough. We loaded Heaven in the car and headed for home.

Pit

She had gotten most of her strength back, to everyone's surprise. Now that she was able to get around, I began to let Rambo come around his daughter a little more.

The first day I let him run around off his chain while she was outside with me. I wasn't sure how he would react to her but I let him get close to her anyway. I held her in my arms as he ran up to me and began to sniff her. She sniffed him back and he started to lick her face. I put her down on the ground and the both of them began to play. I don't know if he realized that this was his daughter but he was very gentle with her.

I did this for about a week before I decided it was all right to take her for a walk with us. The first time I walked both dogs I only walked around the block, but it was still

Pit

pretty hectic. The leashes got tangled and it just became a big mess. After a while they got better and our walks got longer.

One day while walking in the park I ran into Officer Davis. "Hi, John, how are you?"

"I'm doing fine, Larry. Who is this fine little puppy you have with Rambo?"

"This is Rambo's daughter, Heaven."

John looked her over with a smile on his face. Then his smile disappeared. "Oh, she must be from the litter that Mr. Jerry's dog had. It's a shame what happened to those dogs. I didn't know there was a puppy that survived that attack."

I was a little surprised that he knew about the attack but I guess word got around.

Pit

"Yeah, she was in pretty bad shape but I took care of her and she's doing okay now," I said with a look of pride.

John had a pretty serious look on his face and I couldn't help but wonder what was on his mind. "I didn't know that Rambo was the father. I guess you didn't realize what would have become of those puppies had they lived. They would have ended up fighting for Mr. Jerry in the pit."

If it hadn't come from a police officer's mouth, I wouldn't have believed it. "But Mr. Jerry told me that he would never fight dogs nor sell them to anyone who did."

John looked at me as if he knew that the wool had been pulled over my eyes. "Larry, he lied to you, man. Mr. Jerry is one of the biggest dog

Pit

fighters around. He's been doing it for years and he's been to jail for it too. His dogs were probably attacked because he owed someone money or his competitors didn't want to see him at the pit anymore. For your own safety, I would advise you to stay away from Mr. Jerry."

I couldn't believe it. Mr. Jerry was an adult. I had never been lied to by an adult before. I couldn't believe that I had trusted him. I said goodbye to John and went home. From then on I avoided Mr. Jerry.

A few weeks had passed and Heaven was strong and healthy. She was growing so fast that you would never have known she had been the runt of the litter. She and Rambo had grown to be very close and the two of them would play for hours.

Pit

One day while letting her and Rambo run around the yard, I noticed my father standing in the door with a grim look on his face. He came outside and stood next to me. That look on his face told me there was bad news to follow.

"Son, I found a new home for Heaven."

My heart sank and for a few seconds I couldn't say anything. Then with a lump in my throat I asked the question that I already knew the answer to.

"Dad, can we please keep her?"

I cringed as my father replied, "You know the deal we made when we took her. We have to stand by it. I'm proud of the job you did raising her. We really didn't think she would make it. Even Dr. Williams had her doubts. But you hung in there with her. Now you've got to let her go."

Pit

I had grown deeply attached to her, but deep down I knew that my father was right.

"Your cousin has been wanting a puppy for a while, so I think she would enjoy having Heaven."

My cousin Andrea was very nice and I knew that Heaven would be in good hands. We loaded Heaven in the car and took her to my cousin's house. The whole trip Heaven was just as playful as ever. I don't think she had a clue that we were taking her to a new home. We arrived at my cousin's house, where she and my uncle were standing in the yard.

We got out the car and Andrea saw Heaven for the first time. I let Heaven go and she ran straight to Andrea's arms. After seeing that, I knew that she was going to be all right. After giving my cousin feeding

Pit

and caring instructions, my father and I left for home.

Last Experience

Pit

Summer was here again and it seemed that everyone had a dog. Some were new puppies and others were just another year older. As for Rambo, he seemed to know that a new season was upon us and he couldn't wait to get out and about. With the good warm days of summer came some of the bad things that people get into. Word around the neighborhood was that pit fighting was a big thing and a lot of guys couldn't wait to get some action.

Rambo and I took walks in the park almost every day. We tried to avoid the dog-fighting hype that stretched through the neighborhood.

One afternoon a friend of mine came by the house to see me. His name was Eric. The only strange thing about this was that I would usually only see him when I went to his

Pit

house. It had been a long time since he had come to my house and I was quite surprised.

"Hey, man, what are you doing over this way?" I couldn't help but notice that he was in a rush.

"I'm on my way home from my aunt's house." We stood by the old pine tree in the front yard. "I thought I'd come by and tell you about the picnic in the park this weekend."

It was just then when my father called to me from the backyard, "Hey, Larry, I just let Rambo off his chain to run around and get some exercise."

I had turned around to acknowledge my dad when Rambo came trotting toward me. I turned back around to finish my conversation with Eric and he had disappeared.

After hearing some rustling going on above me, I looked up to find Eric hanging from a tree limb. His eyes

Pit

were as big as half-dollars. Eric wasn't a small kid and the way that limb was bent, I didn't know how long it would be before it broke.

"Man, ya… you need to get your dog, man."

I couldn't help laughing. "How the hell did you get up there? He won't bite."

Eric shook his head. "If he's got teeth, then he'll bite."

By now my father had walked to the front yard and noticed Eric hanging onto this tree limb for dear life. "Boy, if you don't get the hell out of my tree—"

I interrupted my dad before he could get too upset. "Dad, he's scared of Rambo. I don't know how he got up there, but he ain't comin' down."

At this point my dad lost it and went into an uncontrollable laugh.

119

Pit

Eric was just as serious as a heart attack. "Mr. Harry, I ain't comin' down until that dog is tied up somewhere."

I took Rambo and put him back on his chain until Eric left. I didn't know that Eric had a dog phobia. I guess that was why he never came around. Eric didn't even finish telling me about Saturday. By the time I came back to the front yard, he was gone.

That Saturday there was a big picnic for the neighborhood held at the park. The local police station hosted the picnic and John was one of the officers in charge. There were all kinds of games and contests for everyone, including the dogs. I entered Rambo in the best-looking dog contest. There were six other entries and Rambo and I took second place. I was so proud of him and he looked as though he was pleased with himself.

John himself had a new German shepherd puppy and he was busy trying to keep her out of trouble.

"So how is everything going, Larry?"

"I'm doing just great. Rambo just took second in the best-looking dog contest."

"He sure has grown," he said as he looked at Rambo with a concerned face.

"He sure has," I agreed.

"Make sure you keep an eye on him. We have been getting a lot of cases of stolen dogs."

I took a great interest in what John was talking about. I didn't know if he was aware of what was happening to those stolen dogs.

"You can help me out," he said. "If you see anything out of the

Pit

ordinary, just give me a call. This is the number to my desk."

John was a close friend but I knew that I couldn't rat anybody out. I took his number, wished him well, and went home.

That night Rambo barked unusually loud for a few minutes but after a while it stopped. I went to sleep feeling that everything was okay. But it wasn't.

The next morning when I woke up and went out to feed Rambo he was gone. My first thought was that he had somehow gotten off his chain. For a while I yelled out his name in the hope that he would come running back, but he never did.

My father came out of the house and noticed that I was beginning to get upset. After looking over the situation, my father realized that Rambo had been stolen. There was a

Pit

small bit of rat poison left around his food bowl. It wasn't enough to kill him but enough to make him weak.

I walked around the whole neighborhood looking for him. Hours went by and I was getting tired. I looked for him all day. I couldn't give up on him. It was getting to be late afternoon when I ran into my friend Eric. He knew about the pit also, but like me he was totally against it.

"A few days ago I heard through the grapevine that Mike had your dog targeted. I'm pretty sure that he was the one who stole your dog."

I ran all the way back home and called John but he wasn't in. I left a message on his machine and gave him a description of where the pit was located. From there I knew where I had to go. I knew that it wouldn't be

Pit

long before the fights would start
and I had to hurry.

Meanwhile at the pit, the fights
were beginning to start. Mike was
anxious to try out his new prize, so
Rambo would fight first. Mike took
Rambo in, holding him by his scruff.
This whole ordeal was new to Rambo
and he didn't have a clue what was
about to take place. His opponent was
Vicious, and even though he was a lot
older, his experience made him one of
the most respected fighters in the
pit.

The men were all screaming and
yelling Rambo's name but after a
while the look of uncertainty on
Rambo's face gave them the impression
that he would be killed very quickly.
With both dogs held by their owners,
Vicious looked to be the more

experienced dog as he snarled and growled.

The whistle sounded and both dogs were turned loose on each other. Immediately, Vicious was the aggressor.

Rambo had never been in this situation before and he looked as though he was refusing to fight. Rambo's peaceful tactics were of no concern to Vicious as he put on the attack. He lunged at Rambo and bit him in the side.

Rambo, still unwilling to fight, got away from Vicious' grip and ran to the opposite side of the cage. But Vicious was relentless in his attack. Dust rose from the cage as Vicious ran at Rambo in a growling rage. He grabbed Rambo by his right hind leg and this time Rambo couldn't escape his grip.

Pit

By this time I was entering the edge of the woods. I could hear Rambo's unmistakable whine as he lay helpless in Vicious' grasp. Then, as though the instinct for survival kicked in, Rambo's whine turned into a ferocious growl. He reached down and locked Vicious' face into his big jaws.

Vicious could not keep his hold on Rambo and both dogs let go.

I reached the edge of the pit and what I saw from then on was very unnerving. As I started running down toward the cage, I began crying out and yelling, "Stop! No!"

Both dogs stood in the middle of the pit staring each other down and growling in rage. They were circling each other and Rambo had a slight limp. Vicious jumped up and lunged at Rambo. Somehow Rambo had gotten

Pit

underneath and pretty soon he had Vicious' neck locked in a death grip.

The men began chanting, "Kill, kill, kill…."

I reached the cage and in a scared voice I screamed at the top of my lungs "No! Rambo, stop!"

The sound of my voice made everyone quiet. Rambo looked up at me with those brown puppy eyes and released his grip. His pretty white coat was red from bloodstains. He walked over to the edge of the cage where I was kneeling and sat next to the cage so that I could reach him.

Vicious, although not dead, was seriously injured and just lay there. I reached my hand through the cage and began stroking Rambo's head. That familiar whimper of his made my heart melt and I began to cry.

Pit

"Everything's going to be all right, boy."

He was weak and frail from the ordeal he had just gone through. Off in the distance I could hear the sound of police sirens. John must have gotten my message.

The spectators wasted no time in gathering up all of their drugs and paraphernalia and scattering through the woods.

Mike was already a big name with the law. Surprisingly he didn't try to get away initially. I guess in his sick, insane mind he felt that he needed to get rid of some, if not all, of the evidence. He took out his 9mm pistol and began making his way into the cage. He pointed the gun at Vicious and shot him in the back of the head.

Pit

I looked at him in disgust. "You are one sick motherfucker. You're gonna pay for this shit."

He looked at me with those sick eyes and I could tell that he was high. "What you talkin' bout, man? I'm a minor; they can't do shit to me. Of course, you know I ain't done yet."

He raised his gun again. I couldn't believe what I was seeing. Everything seemed to be happening in slow motion. He pulled the trigger and the lethal bullet hit Rambo in the side of the head. His blood splashed up on my shirt.

I yelled at the top of my lungs, "No!"

Mike took off running, but before he could reach the top of the hill, the police caught him from behind and took him into custody. Rambo was dead. I was devastated.

Pit

A few days passed and everything turned out just like Mike said— nothing happened to him. Word around the neighborhood was that he was out and picking up right where he left off.

Knowing that he was out made me even more furious. I wanted revenge and would take the law into my own hands if I had to.

That afternoon I went out looking for him. I checked his house first but deep down I knew where I could find him.

He wasn't home, and although it would be very hard for me, I knew I would have to go back to the pit. I started my journey and got to the edge of the wooded area before I stopped. I could hear in the distance what sounded like the growl of a dog and the slashing of a whip.

I continued through the woods and stopped at a tree near the edge of the pit. Hiding behind the tree, I looked down into the pit and there was Mike with one of his new dogs. It was the new female rottweiler, Joan of Ark. She was a little older, maybe a year old, and she was pregnant.

He had her tied on the short chain and he was beating her with a leather belt. With every stroke she got meaner and meaner. She wouldn't be able to stand much more and the sight of it made me want to kill him. Her rage grew with each stroke and so did mine.

He cursed at her and called her names with every stroke. "You dumb bitch! Who told you to go off and get pregnant? You got pregnant by some stupid neighborhood mutt. I'll never be able to get rid of those fuckin' mutt puppies. You no good dirty bitch!"

I couldn't take it anymore. Just as I started to run down, the unthinkable happened.

In her incredible rage, Joan broke the chain. With a look of shock on his face, Mike immediately took off running, but he didn't get far. First she caught him by the right thigh and brought him to the ground. Her killer instincts kicked in and she locked her huge jaws around his neck.

Mike struggled for a few seconds but Joan's rage and strength were too much for him. After the struggle was over, she let him go. Mike was dead.

Continuing His Legacy

Pit

Days and even months passed, yet my heart was still heavy from the loss of my best friend. I couldn't eat and to sleep only gave me nightmares about the pit.

One day, when my father noticed that I was feeling as low as I would probably ever feel, he sat me down and began to console me in the best way he knew how.

"Larry, I know that you are in a great deal of pain, but Rambo is in a better place right now. He would want you to move on with your life. Besides I want you to come with me. I have a surprise for you."

We got into the car and my father took me to a place that I hadn't been in a long time. We went to my cousin's house.

I don't think I'd been there since we had given Heaven to Andrea. We got out of the car and were greeted at the door by my uncle.

"Andrea is in the backyard with the puppies."

I looked up at my dad. "You mean Heaven had puppies?"

My father smiled. "Surprise, son."

I ran through the house passing by my aunt on the way. Andrea was outside with Heaven and the new puppies.

"What's up, coz? I see Heaven had a nice litter."

Heaven was a nice healthy pit bull with a beautiful litter of eight puppies.

"She had nine but one died last night," Andrea said.

By now my father and uncle joined us outside.

"Larry, your father told me what happened to Rambo. We are very sorry about that. You know that you are

Pit

more than welcome to take one of these puppies if you want one."

I thought about it for a while, and even though I felt a little better, I wasn't ready to have another dog. But it was nice to know that Rambo's legacy would live on.

"Thank you, Uncle Lewis, but I think I'll wait before I get another dog."

I didn't think the wait would be this long. I am now thirty-one years old and to this day I've never had another dog. Some friends are hard to replace.

Even though my best friend happened to be a dog, he was still the sweetest gift. I always knew that he would never get away from me, nor want to, nor try to.

Pit

I would definitely like to dedicate this story to my fraternity brothers in purple and gold. More than anything our organization is built on friendship.

Pit

Dedications and Thanks

Dedicated to the memory of my childhood best friend. Rest in peace

Special thanks to my mother for her inspiration in writing this book.

Thanks to my father for your guidance in raising a wonderful dog.

Thanks to my brothers Harry and Chris for their ongoing support.

To my daughters Nikki and Siarrah, I love you very much.

Book cover designed by
Mike Cox
Alpha Advertising
http://alphaadvertising.com/covers
mike@alphaadvertising.com

Printed in the United States
18180LVS00002BA/1-99

9 781414 003931